Dracula in Sunlight

Some more Young Lions you will enjoy

CHRIS POWLING

Dracula in Sunlight

Illustrated by Robert Geary

Young Lions
An Imprint of HarperCollinsPublishers

First published by Blackie & Sons Ltd 1990
First published in Young Lions 1992

Young Lions is an imprint of
HarperCollins Children's Books,
a division of HarperCollins Publishers Ltd,
77–85 Fulham Palace Road,
Hammersmith, London W6 8JB

Printed and bound in Great Britain by
HarperCollins Manufacturing, Glasgow

Contents

Another one for Jan.
Who else?

1   Once Forever After

What I love best in the world are stories.

Stories, yes.

And I don't just mean reading them or listening to them on my Walkman. Most of all I love *telling* them. That's why my twin brother Pip and my little sister Nicky got one of my stories every night at bedtime . . . whether they wanted it or not. They couldn't stop me, you see, because we shared the same room. Our beds were so close together I didn't even have to raise my voice. In fact, it was *dangerous* to raise my voice because if Mum heard from downstairs she used to bang on the kitchen ceiling with a broom – knock! knock! knock! – meaning *go to sleep*.

Sleep?

When there were stories to be told?

Night after night I came up with a new one – about Dracula Dust, for instance, which according to me gathered bit by bit on upstairs window-sills waiting for rain at midnight to turn it into a vampire.

'Like our window-sill?' Nicky squeaked. 'You mean there's Dracula Dust on our window-sill?'

7

'Especially *our* window-sill,' said Pip. 'But don't let it bother you, Nicky. Twelve o'clock's at least five minutes away and there's no rain about tonight . . . I think. Hey, is that pitter-pattering I can hear?'

'Aaaaaaagh!' went Nicky.

This got us three knocks on the ceiling, naturally. Also a shout up the stairs from Dad saying he'd be up to warm our backsides for us if we didn't pack it in. Didn't we know we had school tomorrow?

We knew that all right. 'Flippin' school,' muttered Pip. 'We've got it every day, practically.'

'Yeah,' said Nicky. 'Except for Saturday and Sunday and you have to wait all flippin' week for those.'

I said nothing. I was too cross with the pair of them. This was the third night in a row I didn't dare go on with my story because they'd managed to tip off Mum and Dad. It was almost as if they'd done it on purpose.

On purpose?

No . . . they wouldn't have.

Would they?

I decided to play safe. The following night, just in case, there'd be no Dracula or suchlike to give them the chance to fake being frightened. Instead, I'd offer them a *daft* story. And to convince Mum and Dad we were asleep, I'd leave a long gap before I began.

Too long for Pip, apparently. 'Aren't we having a story, Kath?' he yawned as soon as we were in bed.

'In a minute,' I said.

'I'll be sleepy by then,' said Nicky.

'Me too,' said Pip.

Loudly, he pretended to snore. Nicky joined in at once. Soon their snores and whistles were deafening – the whole room seemed to echo with them. 'OK, OK,' I said hastily. 'No need to be sarcastic.'

'Snore-castic, you mean,' said Nicky.

'Yeah,' giggled Pip. 'Snore-castic is what we're being.'

'Just belt up and I'll start,' I said.

'Snore you're ready?' asked Nicky.

'I expect Kath's just getting herself snore-ganised,' Pip added.

I gritted my teeth. So they were in that sort of mood, were they? All the better to appreciate a daft snory – I mean story. I'd start straightaway, regardless.

Almost at once I knew it was a mistake. This story was about a cat born with a beak instead of a mouth. Every time you gave it some milk it went quack-quack-quack instead of miaow-miaow-miaow. Nicky and Pip thought this was hilarious. They laughed so much I was worried they'd wet themselves.

'All right, all right,' I said. 'It's not that funny. I haven't even got to the bit where the cat lays an egg yet.'

'An egg?' spluttered Nicky. And with a great hoot of mirth, she bounced about on her mattress as if it were a trampoline.

'Careful,' I hissed. 'Any second now and you'll —'

Too late. It happened that second exactly. With a huge BOING of bedsprings, Nicky vanished down the gap between her bed and mine.

KERBONK!

Of course, it was too dark for us to see what she'd done. We could hear it, though. And so could Mum and Dad. No sooner had the thud of Nicky's crash-landing died away than the whole house quaked all over again from heavy footsteps on the stairs. The bedroom door banged back and a door-shaped shaft of light split the bedroom in two.

'What's going on up here?' Dad demanded.

'Dad,' whimpered Nicky in her best baby-of-the-family voice. 'I fell out of bed.'

Somehow she got away with it as usual. But not before we'd all been threatened with having our beds swopped for cots, with early nights for the rest of the century, and with a million-plus-one reminders that tomorrow was a school-day. 'As if we didn't know,' I groaned. 'School-school-school is all they think about.'

'Bet if Nicky had broken her neck they'd still send her to school,' Pip said. 'I notice you didn't say a dicky-bird when we were being told off, Kath. Cat got your tongue, has it?'

'The cat with the beak?' Nicky sniggered.

I snatched at the bedclothes and turned over without answering. Now I was convinced Pip and Nicky had hatched some sort of plot to wreck my story-telling.

Why though?

Jealousy, was it? Or maybe just a joke to get my

wild up? Either way I wasn't the kind of kid to let them get away with it. I'd go on telling stories at bedtime as long as I wanted to . . . forever if necessary.

Forever?

Well, nearly forever. Till I ran out of ideas, anyway. But when it came to stories I had so many ideas queuing up in my brain I couldn't see that ever happening. What I needed now was a batch of tales that weren't too jokey or scary so Nicky and Pip had no excuse to muck me about. I'd better choose them carefully . . .

Which is what I did. All next day. Miss Maynard, our class teacher, nearly nagged me skinny for being so absent-minded but I just didn't care so long as I was ready to get back on top with my story-telling.

That night, to my surprise, my first story went down really well. 'Good stuff, Kath,' Pip said when I'd finished.

'Another one, please,' said Nicky.

'OK,' I said.

My tale of King Arthur come alive again in the Wild West had already taken half an hour. So now I added two more adventures in which Sir Lancelot met Big Chief Sitting Bull and Billy the Kid fell in love with Queen Guinevere. They liked these too. Or Pip did, anyhow. Nicky seemed to be asleep for most of them. Right at the end she woke up so suddenly it was as if one of us had kicked her. 'Terrific,' she mumbled. 'Let's have one more.'

'One more?'

'You're on top form tonight, Kath.'

'Am I?'

'Sure you are.'

After that my story of how Indiana Jones also joined the Round Table was bound to be a success. I told it three times altogether – the best version being the one where Sir Mordred tied himself in a knot while trying to steal Indiana Jones's famous whip. 'He'd have been crippled for life if it hadn't been for his armour,' I explained.

'Serve him right,' Nicky yawned. 'Let's hear it again.'

Or was it Pip doing the yawning? It was hard to tell in the dark with our voices kept carefully below Mum-and-Dad-level. Anyway, what did it matter? So long as one of them paid attention and told me how good I was afterwards, I didn't care if they took it in turns to listen.

Version number four – told from the viewpoint of Indiana Jones's horse – was absolutely brilliant according to Pip. Yes, definitely Pip. 'How about another story, Kath?' he asked. 'Tell it four different ways just like the last one.'

I smiled modestly in the darkness. 'If you really want me to, Pip.'

'Of course I do.'

'Aren't you getting a bit tired?'

'With Kath Satchwell's story-telling? No way!'

He sounded a bit tired, though. Half-way through my next set of stories I could have sworn it was his breathing I heard, not Nicky's. By the end it was clearly Nicky who'd taken over as the listener. 'Smashing story, Kath,' she said straight away. 'Go on.'

'Go on?'

'With your stories. You haven't run out, have you?'

'Who me? I've got millions of them.'

'No problem, then.'

'No problem,' I agreed.

'Good.'

Nicky sounded so keen I still didn't suspect anything. I was well into the tale of Sir E.T., the only extra-terrestrial ever to be knighted by King Arthur, before I realised what the scuffling sound had been between Nicky's bed and Pip's. Nicky had kicked Pip awake again before she snuggled down herself.

They *were* taking turns to listen!

Like sentries on guard-duty they'd set up a rota – a half-hour on and half-hour off, each alternating with the other. They could go on all night like this. Clearly they *meant* to go on all night like this. Or till they'd tired me out, of course. I'd fallen head first into their trap.

I was so furious I described how E.T. had a mad fit and laser-beamed Sir Galahad. 'Sir Galahad?' Pip objected at once. 'Wasn't he the really good knight?'

'The perfect knight,' I snarled. 'And that was just the start of it.' I was about to continue with the wiping out of the entire Round Table when I realised this would stop my story in its tracks. Wasn't that exactly what they wanted? I swallowed hard and took a deep breath. 'Just the start of it . . .' I repeated.

Did Pip groan at this point? If not, it wouldn't be long before he did. Nicky, too, before I was finished. Because I wasn't going to finish. I'd see them both asleep before I did that. I'd go on and on and on . . .

It wasn't easy, I can tell you. Sometimes my words got as slow and dull as the tick of the clock in the hall downstairs. Sometimes they speeded up to a gabble as I rushed to stay awake. Once, so weary I could hardly move my lips, never mind my brain, I pushed back the blanket and shuffled robot-like to the window, muttering over my shoulder at whichever of them was listening. I remember the way the world looked when I took a peek outside – backyards and buildings so gloomy and still they seemed carved from Dracula Dust. Not

15

even a cat with a beak moved through the greyness.

Greyness?

Was dawn that close?

How much longer before we had to get up, then? Could I be that near to winning? Or losing?

I staggered back to bed wondering if my tongue really was as worn out as it felt. By now it didn't seem to matter very much what happened in my story as long as something did. For all I cared Brer Rabbit could be King of Camelot. Or Superman. Or Father Christmas. Maybe the three of them took it in turns – lobbing Arthur's crown from one to the other like kids playing pass-the-parcel. This idea was the last thing I can remember before my eyes finally drifted shut.

Well, not quite the last thing. The last thing was Pip and Nicky. They were both awake now. 'Good-night, Kath,' I heard them giggle.

They were still giggling when I woke up about ten seconds later. Well, that's how long it seemed to me. Mum was pulling back the curtains, filling the room with winter sunshine. 'What's so funny?' she demanded.

'Nothing,' said Nicky and Pip together.

But she'd already noticed the way they were smirking at me. 'Anything wrong, Kath?' she asked.

I shook my head. Why get them into trouble? They'd beaten me fair and square after all. Mum looked at me suspiciously. 'Are you sure you're all right? From the colour of you, you haven't had a wink of sleep.'

This creased up Pip and Nicky, you can bet. Mum glared at them shrivellingly, reaching across Pip's head to test my forehead with the flat of her hand. 'No temperature,' she said. 'How do you feel?'

Tired out, I wanted to reply. She'd have asked why, though, so instead I said, 'Not too bad, I suppose.'

At least, that's what I tried to say. All that came out of my mouth was a tiny squeak. 'You've lost your voice, young lady,' Mum said briskly. 'Got a bit of a chill, probably. No school for you today.'

'What?' said Pip.

'Hey!' exclaimed Nicky.

'As for you two, get yourselves dressed and downstairs for breakfast in five minutes sharp,' Mum
snapped. 'I don't take very kindly to a couple of kids
who laugh when their sister's not well. So get a move
on the pair of you.'

Already she was fussing up my bedclothes to make
me comfy. 'It's not serious, Kath,' she assured me. 'No
need to bother the doctor, even. A day at home is all
you need – you'll be as right as rain tomorrow. And
don't fret about that old dragon, Miss Maynard. I'll
give the other two a note for her. OK?'

'OK,' I squawked.

Behind her I saw Pip and Nicky looking stunned as
they got out of bed. I settled back on the pillow
struggling hard to keep my face straight. 'Mum,' I
managed to whisper.

'Yes, Kath?'

'I think I know what I can do today.'

'It had better not strain that voice of yours.'

'Oh, it won't,' I promised her. 'I shan't say a word
out loud. It all takes place in my head, you see. I'll just
lie here quietly in bed . . . making up stories.'

2   Owning Up

At our school there's a rule you never break. You wouldn't dare – and even if you did you'd be found out quick as a blink. This is the rule about how you stand when you get sent to see the headteacher. It goes like this:

NOSE TO THE WALL IF YOU'VE COME FOR A BAD REASON. *BACK* TO THE WALL IF YOU'VE COME FOR A GOOD REASON.

Get it?

It means Ms Dixon, even though she's new, can tell whether to be cross or smiley the instant she sets eyes on you. That's why we felt so awful as we stood there – all three of us in a row – with our noses practically flat against the shelves outside her room.

'Maybe . . . maybe she'll think it's funny,' I suggested.

'Some hopes,' said Pip.

'Well, she does tell jokes in Assembly, Pip.'

'Not this kind.'

'No,' I admitted. 'Not this kind.'

'Not this kind,' echoed Nicky.

I smothered a groan. In a way it was all my fault since I'd had the idea in the first place. How could I have been so daft? 'Trust Mr Rainbird to spot what we were up to,' I said miserably.

'Never misses a thing, Mr Rainbird,' agreed Pip. 'From the other side of the flippin' classroom as well. Hawk-eyes he's got.'

'Hawk-eyes,' Nicky repeated.

'Shark's eyes, more like,' I said.

With a shark's grin to match in my opinion. I could still see it on his face as he made a circle in the air round the three of us with his finger – then stabbed it in the direction of Ms Dixon's room. You didn't have to be a genius to work out his message. 'It's a trip to Dippy Dixon for you lot,' sniggered a kid on the next table.

'Give her a kiss from us,' laughed another kid.

As we'd slunk through the door, Mr Rainbird called out something after us. His words were lost in all the wet lunch-time hubbub. Not that it mattered. It was a fair cop and we knew it. 'Think she'll be long?' Pip said hoarsely.

'What will she say?' Nicky squealed.

'Dunno,' I said.

But I was telling fibs. We all knew what she'd say — the sort of thing any headteacher would say when she saw a picture like the one we'd drawn. I went hot and cold just thinking about it. Pip, too, judging by the huskiness in his voice. 'Reckon we'll get the cane?' he asked.

I shook my head. 'Not been allowed for years.'

'Will she show what we did to Mum and Dad, then?'

'Maybe,' I swallowed.

'I know what we'll get,' said Nicky. 'She'll chuck us out of the school.'

'No . . . not for a rude picture.'

But could I be sure of that? I wanted to scream out loud. How had I got us into this? And how could I get us out? I shot a quick glance either side of me. Pip was biting his bottom lip so hard it was as if he were trying to eat himself. Nicky was skipping from one foot to the

other with tiny, teeth-gritty whimpers: skip-skip-skip, whimper-whimper-whimper.

'What's the matter?' I asked her.

'Want to go loo, Kath.'

'No, you don't,' I said quickly.

'I do.'

'You just *think* you do.'

'No, I want to. I really want to. I'll be wetting myself soon.'

'Ms Dixon'll love that,' Pip snorted. 'A puddle of you-know-what outside her door.'

'Please, Kath,' Nicky begged.

'OK,' I said. 'I'll nip you down to the girls' toilets.'

'You won't,' snapped Pip. 'That'll leave me on my own.'

'We'll be as quick as we can, Pip.'

'Kath, you won't be any time at all because you're staying right here. Can't she cross her legs or something?'

'I am already,' protested Nicky.

'Great,' Pip snarled.

With a sigh, I decided to be generous. I was mostly to blame, after all. 'You take her, then,' I said to Pip.

'Me?'

'Yes, you. You don't have to go in with her, dimbo. Just wait outside till she's finished.'

'Yeah . . .' Pip said, perking up.

Quickly he grabbed Nicky's hand. 'Won't be long, Kath,' he called over his shoulder.

Liar.

They'd be as long as they possibly could, obviously. Wouldn't I be if I were them? With any luck – their luck – Ms Dixon would arrive ages before they got back. By then I'd have copped the worst of it. What would I tell her? My hand shook as I reached into the pocket of my jeans for the picture.

It was brilliant. Full of detail and neatly coloured-in with my best pentels. No wonder it had taken us every tick of the lunch-time clock to get it finished. We'd even signed it with our names at the bottom. And put a title at the top – a title every kid in the school would recognise from the week before: THE POLITENESS ASSEMBLY.

Except we'd changed one word.

THE RUDENESS ASSEMBLY was what we'd called it.

As I stared at it now, with the February rain beating on the roof and the bell for afternoon school about to ring at any moment, the picture seemed even worse than I remembered. There was our teacher, Miss Maynard, picking her nose with a long, bony finger. There were Mr Rainbird and Mrs Roper having a snog behind the piano. There was Ms Dixon herself, out in front, doing a sort of can-can dance with her skirt lifted high so the whole school could see her knickers . . . and that was just the teachers. The kids were having a pretty rude time, too. I won't tell you how they were carrying on. What excuse could I possibly give?

None, of course.

What I had to do was confess – show her I was so upset she wouldn't have the heart to be strict with us. Wasn't that our only hope?

Almost before I'd made my mind up, Ms Dixon turned the corner. 'Hello, Kath Satchwell,' she said. 'I've been expecting you.'

'Have you?' I said faintly.

'I've just been talking to Mr Rainbird. Where are Nicky and Pip?'

'Gone to the loo, Ms Dixon. But we don't need them – honestly, we don't.'

'Don't we?'

I took a deep breath. 'Mr Rainbird was too far away, miss,' I blurted out. 'He thought it was all three of us. But it wasn't. It was me, mostly. I talked them into it, Ms Dixon. It's down to me, really. I'm the one

who should get done for it.'

'Done for it?'

'Caned, miss,' I said. 'Or expelled.'

'I see,' said Ms Dixon slowly. 'That serious, is it?'

She frowned. Somehow this made her prettier than ever. But when she spoke again her voice was as chilly as the corridor. 'So why have you got your back to the wall instead of your nose, Kath? That's the school rule, I believe.'

'What? Oh – sorry, miss. I was facing the wall, truly. All the time. But just before you came I turned to look at . . . to look at . . .'

'To look at the picture Mr Rainbird mentioned? The one you've been working on with Pip and Nicky since the start of lunch-time?'

Fiercely, I shook my head. 'It was *me*, Ms Dixon. On my own, practically. All my brother and sister did was help me colour it in.'

'Is that the truth?'

'Cross my heart, miss.'

'Then perhaps I'd better take a look at this famous picture. You've brought it with you, I hope?'

I hung my head. 'Yes,' I whispered.

'Let me see it, then.'

As I handed it over I started to sob. They were soft, hiccupy sobs – the kind that really sound convincing. Ms Dixon still took her time with the picture, though. She seemed to be studying every square centimetre of it. 'Very . . . interesting,' she said at last. 'Mr Rainbird told me you were one of our best artists, Kath. I'm

26

sure he's right. Is this really all your own work – apart from the colouring?'

'Yes, miss,' I gulped.

'Imaginative, too. You've never seen Miss Maynard doing this, I hope?'

'No, miss.'

'Or Mr Rainbird and Mrs Roper doing this?'

'No, miss.'

'And I've certainly never danced like this in Assembly – in the draughty old hall we've got, very likely I'd catch my death of cold.'

'No, miss,' I choked. 'I mean – yes, miss.'

By now I was like a big, blubbing jelly. Honestly, I was a mess. Even my hair was sticky with tears. 'The children's behaviour is even worse, I see,' she went on. 'Is this a true picture of our school, Kath?'

'No, miss,' I mumbled.

'So you don't think I should pin up your drawing in my room, then – where no visitor could miss it?'

With our names on it? Where Mum and Dad were certain to hear about it sooner or later? I froze in mid-snivel. 'I don't like that idea, miss,' I wailed.

Behind my back I crossed my fingers.

Just like a headteacher, Ms Dixon made me wait ages for her answer. 'Kath,' she said at last, 'by Monday morning I want another picture – just as good, mind – which I *can* put on my wall. With the proper title this time. It shouldn't take up too much of your weekend if Pip and Nicky help with the colouring. Let me down, though . . . and I'll take this matter further. Do you understand?'

Understand? I couldn't believe we'd been let off so easily. 'Is that all, Ms Dixon?' I gasped.

'All?'

Ms Dixon lifted an eyebrow. 'Aren't you sorry, then?'

'Yes, miss,' I said hastily. 'I really did have my nose to the wall. Honest, I did. So did Pip and Nicky.'

'Good.'

'And I did own up, miss.'

'That's true, yes.'

'Can . . . can I go now, miss?'

'Till Monday, Kath.'

'What? Oh . . . right.'

'Don't forget, Kath. I'll be expecting you.'

I nodded eagerly. 'Bye, miss,' I said.

And that was it. Apart from the smile on her face as Ms Dixon shut her door. A smile, yes. Headteachers can be really weird. If our picture was that funny why was she punishing us at all?

Still, things could've been a lot worse. I pushed my hair into some sort of shape, brushed the wetness from my cheeks and had a good sniff. My brother and sister had better be grateful that my acting was as nifty as my drawing. I was swanking a bit, I admit, as I strolled down the corridor to meet them. They almost knocked me over as they turned the corner. 'Kath! Kath!' Nicky was shrieking.

'Have you seen her?' Pip demanded.

'Ms Dixon?'

'No, the abominable flippin' snowman. Of course, Ms Dixon. We were scared we might not get back in time.'

'Yeah?' I said.

'Yeah,' said Pip. 'You haven't talked to her yet, have you?'

I shrugged. 'No problem. Just a misunderstanding, that's all. We soon sorted it out, Ms Dixon and me.'

'Really?' Pip said.

'Really?' piped up Nicky.

'No sweat,' I told them.

They stared at me, stunned by my coolness. 'How did you guess, then?' Pip asked.

'Guess?'

'About Mr Rainbird.'

'What?'

'We met him,' said Nicky. 'He came out of the staffroom as we went by. He patted Pip on the back. And gave me a kiss on the top of my head. He said we were the best children in the school this lunch-time, Kath. And that's what he'd told Ms Dixon.'

My mouth gaped open. 'He did?'

'Yeah,' grinned Pip. 'Dead lucky we were. He couldn't make out what was *in* our picture, Kath. All he could see was how brilliant it was. So he sent us to Ms Dixon for special praise. Good job you spotted we weren't really in trouble. Could've been nasty, that. Well done!'

'Well done, Kath,' said Nicky.

For a moment I couldn't speak. All I could think

about was the smile on Ms Dixon's face. 'Anything wrong?' Pip asked.

'You OK?' asked Nicky.

I licked my lips. When it came to owning up at least I'd had plenty of practice. 'Er . . . about this weekend,' I began. 'I've thought of something really good we can do . . .'

3   A Family Secret – Part I

One reason I like stories so much is that they *stop* properly. They finish with 'happily ever after' or 'The End' and you feel satisfied as you turn the last page. Real life isn't like that. It's sort of messy. It's like a story that hasn't been sorted out yet – you just go on and on turning over. Till you're dead, I suppose.

This is why I was so fond of my mum and dad's wedding album. It felt like a bit of their life turned into a story. In the last picture, for instance, they're driving away from the reception in a big, fancy old car that's all covered in foam and ribbons and jokey notices. It's a 'happily ever after' picture. To tell you the truth, my mum and dad's wedding album was my favourite book of all till I was about ten years old. I can still remember the day when that changed.

The day when it changed?

I can still remember the *minute* when it changed. The *split-second*, even. Because it was my brother's fault, really. You see, though Pip is my twin he's not a bit like me in some ways. One of those ways is that I'm day-dreamy and he isn't. Pip notices things.

Mind you, he didn't notice our Family Secret for quite a while. To begin with he wasn't even looking at the wedding album. Mostly he was moaning about Nicky. 'She's a real dimbo,' he said.

I shrugged. 'She's only six.'

'Yeah, but a baby-ish six. Look where she is this morning – playgroup. Playgroup? At six years old? You leave playgroup when you start school, right? Not Nicky! Every time we get a day off she goes back there!'

'To help,' I said.

'Aged six?'

'Mum says she's terrific, Pip. Especially with the shy ones and the really little kids. All the toddlers trust Nicky, Mum says.'

'She's not much more than a toddler herself,' Pip snorted. 'That's why they trust her.'

'How come they don't trust each other, then?' I asked.

'What?'

I shook my head. It was a waste of time pointing out to Pip he wasn't thinking straight. His real problem was his bad temper with me. I wanted to read and he didn't. The grumbling was to pay me back. Not that I was letting him get away with it. I kept my eyes fixed on the wedding album propped up against my pillow. 'What are you looking at?' he asked.

'Can't you see?' I said.

'Why that thing?'

'It's good.'

'Good?'

'Well, interesting.'

'Wedding pictures? Thinking of getting married, are you?'

'Divorced,' I said.

'What?'

'From you, Pip. If you keep interrupting.'

'You can't divorce your twin,' Pip sniffed.

'I can.'

'Yeah?'

'I'll get the Government to pass a special law,' I said savagely. 'Leave me alone, can't you?'

That shut him up. For about ten seconds, actually. 'How can I be interrupting?' he demanded. 'There aren't any words down there for me to interrupt. You're just staring at photographs, right?'

I sighed. He'd been like this all morning – ever since Mum and Nicky had gone out. Lying on a bed reading was no way to spend a Spring holiday, he reckoned. We should be at the swimming pool. Or out on our roller boots. 'You go,' I suggested.

'On my own? That's no fun.'

'Plenty of other kids will be around.'

'Lucky them,' he sniffed.

And went on fidgeting about on the bed next to mine even though I'd told him a million times I fancied a lazy, browsy day.

I sighed again.

Now he was looking over my shoulder. I knew exactly what he was after – the chance to rubbish whatever picture I'd got to. 'That one?' he sniggered.

It was the picture on the church steps – Mum and Dad in the middle, in their wedding clothes, surrounded by all our uncles and aunts and cousins and grandparents and friends-of-the-family. 'What's the matter with it?' I asked.

'Wrong film in the camera,' Pip said.

'Eh?'

'Should be black and white – white for Mum's family, black for Dad's. No need for a colour picture, right?'

I wanted to kill him. 'That's racist,' I spat.

My disgust made even Pip back off. 'Only a joke,' he said.

'A racist joke,' I snarled. 'What would you do if somebody else came up with it?'

'They'd better not try,' said Pip.

'Exactly.'

He'd got what he wanted, though. Furious, I turned away from his cocky grin. I should've snapped the album shut there and then. If I had, he might never have spotted who was missing from the picture. 'Hey,' he exclaimed.

'Yes?' I said coldly.

His eyes were on the left-hand side of the picture: Dad's relatives. 'That doesn't make sense . . .' he said.

'What doesn't?'

'That.'

He pointed at a kid, a black kid, standing in the front row next to our Auntie Trish, who had her hand

on his shoulder. 'Who do you reckon that is, Kath?' she asked.

'Vernon,' I said. 'Who else?'

Even as a littley, our brilliant cousin Vernon was unmistakable. As usual, he was wrinkling his nose as if to keep his glasses on. From the look on his face he was struggling to work out some really tough maths problem in his head. Auntie Trish, who never lets us forget she's a teacher, was looking down at him proudly the way she always did. 'Typical,' I snorted. 'Vernon's the most important person in the picture according to Auntie Trish.'

'How old is he?' said Pip.

'Vernon? About twelve, I suppose. He's just gone to that posh secondary school, remember?'

'No, not now. I mean in the picture here.'

I still didn't see what was puzzling him. 'Five?' I suggested.

'About that, yes,' Pip nodded.

'So what?'

'Well, he's two years older than us, right?'

'Yes?'

'So where are we?'

'What?'

'Where are we, Kath?' said Pip patiently. 'Because if he's two years older than us, and here he's about five, we must have been *three*. Right?'

'Right,' I said faintly.

'So why aren't we in the picture?'

'We couldn't have been,' I said. 'How can kids go to

36

their parents' wedding? They haven't been born yet.'

'*We* must have been.'

'Well, maybe Mum and Dad had us first and got married later. That does happen . . .'

Pip shook his head. 'So why leave us at home on the wedding day? Someone could have taken us – even babies get taken to weddings. Nicky's been to millions of them.'

'Only two,' I said. 'Years ago when she was a bridesmaid.'

'Aged three,' said Pip.

OK, so he'd made his point. I glared at cousin Vernon in the picture. He was dressed in a school jersey and neatly pressed shorts . . . about five years old, no question. 'That explains the look on his face,' I said.

'What?'

'Vernon's wondering where *we* are.'

Pip laughed at this. I tried to laugh, too. Somehow it didn't come out right. Pip spotted it at once. 'Kath,' he said. 'If you're that bothered about it, we've only got to ask Mum and Dad.'

'No,' I said quickly.

'Why not?'

'They might be upset.'

'You reckon?' Pip shrugged and pulled a face. To him all this was just a detail, an oddity that wasn't worth fussing about. Who cared, anyway?

Me, that's who.

My brain was doing back-flips. How come my twin

37

brother wasn't worried about *why* we'd been left out of Mum and Dad's wedding pictures? Had we been banned from the church for mucking about? Were we sick in hospital – so sick we'd never been told about it? Then again, suppose we'd been kidnapped? Mum and Dad could've got married while they were waiting for the ransom note! Well, it wasn't impossible.

Neither was the worst explanation of the lot.

I hardy dared think about this.

What if . . . what if Mum and Dad weren't our *real* Mum and Dad?

By now my heart was thumping and my hands felt sweaty. Hastily, I snatched them away from the album in case they made smudges. 'You OK?' Pip asked.

'Fine.'

'You look terrible. What's the problem?'

I tried to smile. 'No problem.'

'Could've fooled me. Look, Kath – I know what you're thinking. That maybe we're not actually *theirs*. Maybe this picture proves they adopted us, right?'

So he had worked it out, after all. I gave a shaky nod. 'Right,' I said.

'But we're theirs *now*, Kath. I mean, they *act* like our mum and dad don't they? Why should this picture make any difference?'

I looked at him in astonishment. 'You wouldn't mind being adopted, then?'

'Why should I?'

'But, Pip—'

'Yes?'

'Pip . . .'

My voice trailed away. Why waste more of my breath? I'd never get him to understand. Even though we were twins, in some ways we were a million miles apart. 'Forget it,' I said.

'Already have,' said Pip.

He had, too. Soon he drifted away and I heard him scrabbling around with something in the bathroom next door – a water-bomb, as it turned out.

We spent the rest of the day making a stock of them, then testing each one by dropping it from our bedroom window through the skylight below straight into the sink in the kitchen. Well, more or less straight into the

sink. The telling off we got from Mum and Dad that night about the mess we'd made didn't seem *adopted* at all.

The trouble was, however hard I pretended otherwise, I knew I'd never forget the puzzle of Vernon in the wedding picture. It would keep on nagging at me like a bad tooth. What I couldn't do, you see, was skip over the next three chapters in this book – a bit like fast-forwarding on a video – so I could find the answer to our Family Secret extra quickly. Only a reader, or a viewer, can do that. In real life, whether you want to or not, you just go on and on turning over. . .

4   The Wopsie

I bet you know what I'm talking about when I say wasps are the best school-wreckers ever. This is because every single kid I've ever met expects to be stung the instant a wasp zizzes on the scene. Even the class goody-goody yells 'Aaagh! Aaagh! It's a *wopsie!*' and smacks at the air like a tennis-player gone potty.

So it was quite interesting in a way on the hot dozy afternoon when a wasp flew into the last assembly of term.

Mr Rainbird, the deputy head, was taking it because Ms Dixon was away on a course. We'd sung the hymn and said the prayer and wished goodbye to the big kids going on to secondary school, all with one eye on the clock to see how close we were getting to home-time. Now we'd reached the bit where he was making us promise to be specially sensible in the long weeks ahead. 'Not silly,' he insisted. 'Not careless or cowardly. But *especially sensible.*'

We nodded eagerly. After all, nobody was interested in messing about with the summer holidays so close.

Then the wasp arrived.

An infant noticed it first. Or thought she noticed it –
was that a buzz of wings and a yellow dot near the top
of the wall-bars? 'WOPSIE! WOPSIE!' she pointed.

Mr Rainbird hesitated. He knew all about kids and
wasps. 'Nothing to worry about, dear,' he said
sharply. 'It's only an insect.'

At once the infant burst into tears. This worried the
other infants a lot. They looked at each other ner-
vously. One of them said in a piping voice, 'Has she
been stung?'

'Stung?' asked another.

'Stung!'

'She's been stung!'

'No she hasn't,' snapped Mr Rainbird. 'She's just

making a silly fuss. No one's been stung. It's a *wopsie*, that's all – a wasp, I mean.'

A half-dozen infants were crying now. Their teacher was glaring at Mr Rainbird as if he'd been doing the stinging. The juniors were beginning to be restless, too. A first year stood up suddenly, slapping his hands madly round his head. 'It's in my hair! It's in my hair!'

'No, it's not. It's over here!' a third year called.

'Maybe there's two of them,' someone suggested.

'A swarm,' added someone else. 'Probably it's a swarm.'

However many wasps there were, or none at all, just the idea of them had everyone flailing about. Kids twisted and turned, elbowing each other out of the wasp's way. Mr Rainbird was furious. 'This is ridiculous!' he roared. 'Stop panicking! There's no need for any of this nonsense!'

He was right, of course, but who was going to believe him? Especially when old Mrs Roper, at the piano, reeled back on her stool, knocking a great wodge of music on to the keyboard.

PLINK! PLENK! PLONKETTY-PLUNK!

'What hymn is that?' called one of the juniors.

Most of us thought this incredibly witty. It wasn't funny at all in Mr Rainbird's opinion. 'Whoever said that can take themselves out of the school right away,' he snarled. 'And I mean right away. No, *no* – sit down, all of you. Sit *down*, I say.'

He was so angry he lashed out with his hymn-book

against the wall-bars.

CRACK!

In the crowded hall the sound was like a pistol shot. Every kid snapped to attention, cross-legged. Infants froze in mid-snivel. Even the teachers sat upright in their chairs. There was pindrop silence.

Mr Rainbird blinked.

He felt every eye on him. 'Good,' he said. 'That's good.'

He tapped the hymn-book against his trouser leg, nodding slowly as he scanned the hall from one side to the other. We heard Mrs Roper gently close the piano lid. Somehow this made the quietness even more quiet.

Mr Rainbird took his time. He wasn't going to let anything spoil this moment. 'Not silly?' he pronounced. 'Not careless? Not cowardly?'

He paused to let his words sink in. One or two kids shifted uncomfortably. Mr Rainbird gave a grim smile. '*Specially sensible?*' he continued. 'Is that how you think you've been behaving this afternoon? With the summer holidays only a few minutes away?' Again he paused, before adding, 'If they *are* only a few minutes away . . .'

We stared at him, horror-struck. Can deputy head-teachers really cancel summer holidays? 'I say this,' Mr Rainbird went on, 'because the holidays may be starting a little late this year . . . if I choose to hold an extra assembly at four o'clock.'

This was bad enough.

All over the hall you could almost hear kids holding

their breath. Mr Rainbird had got us and he knew it. 'And I will hold that extra assembly – I promise you I will – if we have any more of this foolishness. Even the slightest hint of it. Do you understand?'

'Sorry, Mr Rainbird,' a few kids murmured.

'Are you?' Mr Rainbird demanded.

He had an I'm-in-charge look on his face now. 'Are you sorry, leavers?'

'Yes, Mr Rainbird.'

'And the rest of you juniors?'

'Yes, Mr Rainbird.'

'What about you infants?'

'Sorry, Mr Rainbird.'

'I should think so, too. You should be ashamed of yourselves, every single one of you. Complete chaos caused by a tiny, little —'

'Er, Mr Rainbird . . .'

The voice came from the top-infant class.

It was Nicky's voice.

My twin-brother Pip and I cringed down in our places. Was our little sister Nicky going to slow up the start of the holidays for the whole school? We'd never live it down. Already Mr Rainbird was glaring in her direction. 'As I was saying —'

'Mr Rainbird . . .'

'No interruptions, please. Every child here—'

'But, Mr Rainbird . . .'

Nicky was on her feet now, her finger pointing. Mr Rainbird gave a snort of irritation. 'What is it, child?'

'The wopsie, Mr Rainbird.'

46

'Yes?'

'It's crawling up your collar . . .'

'What?'

'. . . I think it's going down your neck.'

'Aaaagh! Aaaagh!'

With a giant leap in the air, Mr Rainbird smacked frantically at his neck with the hymn-book – not exactly a headteacherly thing to do as he saw at once. Hastily, he made a rush for the hall-doors calling to Mrs Roper as he passed, 'Play the going-out music, play the going-out music.'

Mrs Roper did her best.

So did Miss Maynard as she sent us back to our rooms class by class. But it was a pretty ragged exit all the same what with teachers making spluttering noises behind their hands and kids smacking hymn-books against their necks. We had silent reading for what was left of the afternoon – or pretended that was what we were doing. It turned out to be the fastest getaway into the Summer holidays we could ever remember.

We were still giggling about it on the way home. 'Did you see his face?' Pip spluttered. 'Old Rainbird looked as if he'd *swallowed* the blinkin' wasp!'

'If there was a wasp,' I said.

'Eh?'

'Well, nobody actually saw it . . . did they, Nicky?'

She had a small, smug grin on her face – her tricky grin Pip called it. He stared at her suspiciously. 'Was there a wasp?' he demanded.

'Two,' said Nicky.

'There were two wopsies?' I exclaimed.

Nicky nodded. From the pocket of her dungarees she pulled a grubby handkerchief which she opened carefully. In it was a wasp – small and crumpled and dead. 'I squashed this one with my hymn-book,' she told us. 'While Mr Rainbird was going on and on about how silly we were being.'

'What about the other wasp?' asked Pip faintly. 'The one that crawled down Mr Rainbird's neck . . . '

Our little sister's grin now was as wide and wicked as the summer holidays stretching ahead. 'That was the one I made up,' she said.

5   Dracula In Sunlight

Our Auntie Em had a house by the Quaggy. This was why we loved staying with her – or Pip and I did, anyway. Nicky wasn't so sure. 'What's so special about the Quaggy?' she asked.

Pip and I looked at each other, despairingly. Would our little sister never grow up? What do you do with a kid so dim she couldn't see the Quaggy was like a hideout and an adventure both at once? For a start grown-ups never went near it. 'The Quaggy?' they'd say, pulling a face. 'There's more stink than water in that old river. Rats, too. You keep clear of the place.'

Keep clear of the place? Pip and I couldn't wait to get there. The Quaggy was a secret, sunken alleyway that stretched through the city for miles and miles – maybe out into the country and down to the sea for all we knew.

But the bit we liked best was close to Auntie Em's.

We'd stand right on the brink of her scruffy garden, look down and gloat. Could any kids be luckier? Twelve feet below us was Quaggy country. OK, so it was only wellington boot deep at most. OK, so it

wasn't much wider than you could spit provided you had the wind with you. And OK so people did dump rubbish in it so you had to watch your step all the time whether you were wading through the weed-coloured water or clumping through the water-coloured weeds. The Quaggy was risky, OK?

That's what made it so exciting.

For Pip and me, that is. Nicky, as I say, wasn't impressed. 'I mean, you're talking like it was the seaside or something,' she grumbled. 'It's not that good.'

'Isn't it?' I said nastily.

'What can you do at the seaside you can't do at the

50

Quaggy?' Pip asked.

'Swim,' said Nicky.

Pip hesitated. Nicky had a point here, but we'd be daft to admit it this early in the argument. Instead Pip laughed drily as if only weird kids, a bit too frog-like for their own good, ever wanted to swim. 'Well, if that's what you want to do . . .'

'I do,' said Nicky at once.

'What's stopping you, then? There's bound to be somewhere you can swim in the Quaggy – if swimming's what you're after.'

He made swimming sound as rude as picking your nose. This didn't put Nicky off at all. 'Where?' she asked.

Pip turned to me, helplessly. 'Plenty of places,' I shrugged. 'You know, beyond the bridge maybe. Round the bend a bit.'

'Yeah, round the bend,' Pip laughed. 'That's where swimmers go.'

'Sandcastles, then,' said Nicky.

'What?'

'Where can I make sandcastles?'

'Nowhere,' snapped Pip. 'You need sand for that. There's no sand near the Quaggy.'

Nicky nodded. 'There is at the seaside, though. That's what I've been saying.'

She turned away as if that was the end of it and she'd won. 'Round the bend,' I called out after her. 'There's bound to be sand round the bend.'

'Probably in the same place you swim,' added Pip.

Nicky wasn't listening. Or maybe she was wondering if Auntie Em had a bucket and spade she could borrow.

Either way Pip and I were glad to be rid of her. Little sisters can get in the way sometimes. In fact, now I come to think about it, quite a lot of the time little sisters can get in the way. I mean, *sandcastles!* 'She'll be sucking a dummy next,' I told Pip.

'Next?' said Pip. 'You mean she's stopped sucking a dummy?'

We laughed a lot at this. It made us feel better about losing the argument.

The Quaggy made us feel better, too.

Getting down to it was tricky, of course, like always. Whoever went over first had to be lowered by the one who stayed on top, gripping hands firmly. True, the ancient gnarled-up oak growing out of the bank was ladder-like in its way, but not much. You could never be sure a branch wouldn't snap off with a crack or the whole tree uproot itself and crash into the Quaggy in a shower of dry, dusty greenery. Pip and I treated it with as much respect as if it were Auntie Em herself stretching out a skinny brown arm to help us. 'Reckon she'd mind?' I asked Pip.

'Who, Auntie Em?'

'Us going down the Quaggy, I mean.'

Pip smiled wrily. 'Reckon she knows already,' he said.

'Yeah?'

'She's not daft, Kath.'

Pip was right. Auntie Em was the kind of grown-up who knew exactly what kids got up to . . . and most of the time let them go on getting up to it. Auntie Em was still a bit of a kid herself. It was why we liked her so much. Probably she'd chosen this house to live in because the Quaggy wound round it.

That's what we told ourselves, anyway. We felt a bit guilty being there, to tell the truth. Especially without Nicky. 'Reckon she'll be all right?' Pip said.

I nodded. 'Gone swimming, I expect. Or making sandcastles.'

'What – round the bend in the river?'

We both looked that way and shivered.

The curve in the Quaggy was spooky, you see. We'd never dared go round it – nor had any other kids so far as we knew. The water got deeper there, it was said. And darker. Also the weeds were thicker, more tangled. Mostly, though, it was the light coming through the overhanging trees that was so scary – for some reason even on the brightest day it was cold and sad like the sun chinking its way into a dungeon.

So, as usual, we turned in the other direction. Here the Quaggy ran more or less straight between houses and yards. There was a wooden bridge, as well, making a perfect jungle gym. We could clamber and splash for hours . . . which is what we did today. We jumped and threw stones and hung upside down from the bridge's struts. We broke off some branches and had a quarter-staff fight taking turns to be Robin Hood and Little John. We converted the bridge into a Star Wars

53

skyship by lashing our branches to it with some string
we found. Then we switched the string and branches
into rods so we could pretend we were fishing for Jaws
the super-shark . . . and all the while we kept looking
back towards the bend in the river. By lunch-time,
after we'd finished Auntie Em's sandwiches, Pip
couldn't stand it any longer. 'How about taking a
look?' he said hoarsely.

'A look?' I said.

'That way. Round the bend.'

'What?'

'Where we've never been,' said Pip.

'Oh . . . that way.'

I was acting cool, still. But Pip wasn't fooled. 'You brave enough?' he asked.

'Me?'

'Yes, you.'

He stood up, already squinting towards the curve in the Quaggy. 'Coming with me, Kath?'

'What's along there, then?'

'That's for us to find out.'

'Now?'

'Why not now?'

I shrugged as if there were so many reasons why not I couldn't be bothered to list them. I knew it was no use, though. We'd been leading up to this all morning. 'OK,' I said finally. My voice was as hoarse as Pip's.

We picked our way back along the Quaggy as if we expected to set off a booby-trap with every step. At Auntie Em's house we paused and looked up. 'Maybe we should be playing with Nicky,' I said.

'Scaredycat,' Pip sniffed.

So we waded on towards the bend.

It closed over us like a badly thatched roof. Sunlight striped the river-bank with bars further and further apart as if a cage were turning into a coffin. The water was deeper as well as darker. 'Knee-high, actually,' I pointed out to Pip.

'Gungey, too,' he said. 'Like soup.'

'Bet it doesn't taste like soup.'

'Quaggy-soup.'

'Yuk!'

'Gonna test it?'

'Not likely.'

'Me neither. Rot your innards this stuff would.'

'Rot the shoes off your feet, too – wellington boots even.'

We were joking but only just. What with the scum and the shadows and the sudden dazzle here and there where the sky broke through, anything seemed possible. The air had a musty, old-book smell to it like a story coming to life after years and years of mouldering on a shelf.

Suddenly, Pip grabbed my arm. 'What's that?' he said, pointing up the bank.

'A hut,' I said. 'An old hut for gardening tools.'

'Yes, I know that. But who'd build one this close to the Quaggy?'

'Maybe it wasn't to begin with. The Quaggy's worn the bank away, see? The hut'll fall in eventually.'

Don't ask me why we were talking in whispers but we were. 'Look,' I went on. 'Someone's worn a track all the way up to it. Recently, I reckon.'

'Who though?'

Something in Pip's voice suggested it couldn't be a normal person. Not in a spot like this. We shuffled forward through the water. 'Hey,' I yelped.

'What's the matter?'

'Look back, Pip. We can't see Auntie Em's.'

'We haven't been able to for ages.'

I hadn't realised. I felt tricked, somehow, as if I'd turned over two pages at once in the story and reached

a frightening bit before I should. What was frightening about an old hut, though?

Then I saw the ashes.

Ashes, definitely.

They'd have blown away if it hadn't been so sheltered here. There was a trail of them, grey and wispy, winding up the slope to the hut. 'Dracula Dust,' I gasped.

'What?'

'Like . . . like Dracula Dust.'

Pip blinked when he saw where I was pointing. 'Yeah,' he said. 'Just like it.'

'Good job I made it up,' I said. 'About Dracula Dust, I mean.'

'Kath, did you really make it up?'

'Course I did. There's no such thing, Pip.'

'Isn't there?'

'Dracula Dust is imaginary. I got it from a story. Well, sort of from a story. You remember – Dracula crumbles to bits if he gets hit by a shaft of sunlight. All I did in my version was sort of tell it the other way round.'

'Yeah, so it turns back into Dracula at midnight . . . charming!'

We grinned at each other as hard as we could. I mean, what a laugh! Everyone knows Dracula doesn't really exist. It was just the Quaggy giving us the heeby-jeebies. 'Maybe . . . maybe we should check, though,' said Pip.

'Check?'

'You know, take a quick peek in the hut. Just to make sure it's only a place where someone dumps old ash. After that we can forget it.'

I realised what Pip was saying. If we didn't make sure everything here was ordinary and everyday we'd go on wondering for ever. This place would never stop haunting us. 'Pip,' I said uneasily, 'suppose we get caught by the person who owns the hut?'

Pip shrugged. 'Who cares? So long as it isn't . . .'

You-know-who, he meant.

I let Pip go ahead of me up the slope. We followed the ash right round the hut as far as its door. Even the doorstep itself was smudged with grey.

'Looks like the hut's been built at the end of an overgrown garden,' I hissed. 'Except those stinging nettles are so tall we can't see any house back there.'

'Good,' said Pip. 'It means they can't see us, either.'

He was inspecting the door. It had no keyhole or padlock. Just a loose catch anyone could lift. Our eyes met. Pip licked his lips. 'OK, Kath?'

'OK,' I said.

The catch clicked up. The door creaked open flooding the hut with sunlight.

Ash was dumped there all right.

Piled against the back wall was a great drift of it like snow that's died of old age instead of melting. Not a smooth drift of ash, though. This had a shape – a definite shape. At one end the mound was like legs, in the middle like arms alongside a body, and at the other end exactly like a head . . . a head with a scooped-out mouth, two dents in place of nostrils and hollow sockets for the cinders where eyes should have been.

Dracula Dust.

Pip made a noise that sounded like gargling. Or was it me making the noise? Maybe it came from both of us. At any rate we were so close together as we backed away from the hut we could've been holding each other's breath. The door swung shut in front of us so slowly we had plenty of time to notice specks of ash dancing in the air above the dead vampire.

Well, what else could it be?

Even Pip couldn't come up with a better explanation though he tried hard enough as we sloshed back to Auntie Em's at top speed. 'What more do you need to prove it?' I demanded. 'A wooden stake through its heart? A silver bullet in its chest?'

'But vampires aren't real, Kath.'

'This one is – or was, anyway. And maybe it'll be real again if it's true about Dracula Dust.'

'Kath, you made that up. You admitted you did.'

'Maybe I told the truth without realising it. That can happen with stories.'

Pip shook his head. 'No,' he said. 'That's loony.'

'But it was the shape of a vampire, wasn't it? You can't deny that, Pip. Every detail from top to toe.'

'Well, not every detail . . .'

'Too much to be accidental, though.'

'Yeah,' Pip nodded. 'Too much to be accidental.'

He frowned, biting his lip. What bothered him was the same thing bothering me. How could we just *ignore* what we'd found? On the other hand how could we go to grown-ups with our tale? They'd tell us we had too much imagination for our own good – that we'd let ourselves get spooked by a pile of old ash. 'Forget it,' they'd say. And we'd take their word for it, of course. Kids always end up believing grown-ups. So bit by bit we *would* forget it . . . leaving Dracula to rise again anytime he liked. Starting with a raid on the Satchwell family, as revenge for disturbing him.

Gloomily, using Auntie Em's tree for handholds and footholds, we helped each other up the bank of the Quaggy. Sitting cross-legged at the top was Nicky. She seemed wonderfully normal compared with what we'd just seen. 'Hi, Kath,' she called. 'Hi, Pip.'

'Hi, Nicky,' I swallowed. 'Everything OK?'

'Brilliant,' said Nicky. 'I've had a brilliant time. I went where you told me – you know, round the bend in the river where there's swimming and sandcastles.'

Pip and I looked at each other. 'What?' I said.

'That way,' Nicky pointed. 'Course, you can't swim too much 'cos it's mucky. But there's a tiny, tiny house right on the river-bank. Full of this flaky old sand . . .'

I froze. Had my little sister been bitten already? Should I check her neck for tooth marks? 'Did you . . . did you go into the house?' I asked.

'You betcha,' said Nicky, happily. 'I made sand-castles and stuff all morning. And you know what I did to finish?'

'No?'

'I made a shape like I'd buried Daddy – you know,

61

the way we did at the beach last summer. With legs and arms and a body and a head and these cindery-things for eyes. It took hours, Kath. But it looked really, really real . . . you should've seen it!'

Nicky's voice died away as she remembered the fun she'd had. Or maybe she went on talking and it was our listening that died away. All I know is that Pip and I didn't dare say a word to each other for ages.

6 Geronimo

Deep down, everyone knew it wasn't possible to win at Geronimo.

Not the way we played it anyway. Geronimo is the kind of game that varies from kid to kid, but with us the rules were simple. Mostly it was like hide-and-seek. One person scuttled off while the others counted to a hundred. Then it was up to the others to do the finding. But in total silence. They could only communicate by using signals – especially when they felt they'd spotted the hider. If they had, they surrounded their victim as nippily as they could, but still without a word. Then, when everyone was in position, they yelled:

GERONIMO!

And the game was over. The hider was dead.

Unless, of course, you chose to make a run for it. But what sensible kid would do that? In our Geronimo, you see, this gave everyone else the right to chase after you till you'd been caught. Then they all jumped on top of you at once.

POW!

POW!

POW!

Only an idiot or the world's fastest runner took that sort of risk. 'I would,' said our little sister, Nicky.

'Don't be daft,' said Pip. 'You're not the world's fastest runner.'

'Yeah,' I said. 'But she is an idiot.'

'No, I'm not,' Nicky sulked. 'I'm just little. That means there's not as much for you to jump on top of. So it can't be as bad for me, right?

We weren't sure about this. It sounded logical enough, but there was something which didn't quite make sense.

Still, what was the point of arguing when Nicky was too titchy to play a tough game like Geronimo anyway? 'I'm not,' she protested.

'You are,' I said. 'You'll end up all weepy and waily and get Pip and me into trouble.'

'I won't, Kath. Really, I won't.'

'Bet you will.'

'Won't.'

'Will.'

'Won't.'

'Will.'

'Won't,' said Nicky, stamping her foot.

'See?' said Pip. 'Already it's getting stupid. You're too young and that's that.'

At this, Nicky's face crumpled. If we didn't back off she'd end up all weepy and waily whether we played

Geronimo or not.

'Anyway, there's only three of us,' I pointed out. 'You can't play Geronimo properly with only three kids.'

'That's just cos' you don't want me to play,' Nicky sobbed. 'It's not fair.'

Mum and Dad wouldn't think it was fair either. Pip and I could see that. We scowled and shook our heads at each other despairingly. Weren't little kids *awful*. 'Could we?' Pip asked. 'Just a bit of a game, maybe? What do you think, Kath?'

I shrugged. A bit of a game couldn't do much harm, could it? Here we were in the woods, after all. And Mum and Dad were busy snoozing after our picnic. 'We'd have to get the rules straight first,' I said, grudgingly.

'Yeah!' said Nicky. 'Teach me the rules, first.'

'Thought you knew them.'

'Not straight, Kath.'

You could say that again. Nicky's idea of Geronimo was so jumbled it was hard to sort out what she did understand from what she didn't. Even after we'd started playing she got it muddled up. 'Geronimo! Geronimo!' she kept calling when we went looking for Pip.

'Quiet,' I snarled. 'You're supposed to keep quiet.'

'But I like calling out.'

'You don't call out till you've found him.'

'But we haven't found him yet.'

'I know we haven't. That's why we've got to keep

quiet – so we can sneak up on him. If he hears us coming he'll creep away to another hiding place. You don't let him know you've seen him till the last possible moment, get it? That's when you shout.'

'Only then?'

'Right.'

'That's boring,' said Nicky. 'I'd rather play it my way.'

'Well, we wouldn't,' I insisted. 'The game gets ruined.'

It was just the same when it was her turn to hide. Pip and I hadn't even counted to fifty let alone a hundred before we heard Nicky's squeaky voice shouting, 'Geronimo! Geronimo!'

'What's she doing?' Pip said.

'Don't ask me.'

Apparently she thought we needed some help. 'I was waving, too,' she explained. 'So you didn't go in the wrong direction.'

'But we're *supposed* to go off in the wrong direction.'

'Are you?' said Nicky. 'I thought you were trying to find me.'

'We are.'

'Why do you want to go in the wrong direction, then?'

'We don't *want* to go in the wrong direction, you twerp. But if we do it's easier for you to stay hidden. That's the whole point of the game.'

Nicky looked at us blankly. 'You mean you're trying to help me stay hidden?'

'Of course not, dimbo. We're trying to track you down.'

'I know,' said Nicky. 'That's why I was waving and calling out. So we could get to the best bit quickly – where we call out "Geroniomo"!'

'We don't all call it out,' I snapped. 'Just Pip and me.'

'Not me?'

'No – you're the hider. Only the seekers call out.'

'But I kept calling when I was a seeker, Kath. You told me to shut up because it was ruining the game.'

See what I mean? We had to go right back to the beginning and explain the rules again. And again. Even then I wasn't sure she'd got the hang of it. 'This is a soppy game,' she said.

But when we offered to drop the whole thing her chin trembled and her eyes filled with tears. 'Want to play Geronimo,' she told us.

I ask you. Who'd have a little sister?

At last, with half the afternoon over, she seemed to have sorted it out. 'You mustn't find me, right? I stay secret as long as I can.'

'Right,' said Pip.

'And the game isn't over till you've found me and you've called out Geronimo, right?'

'Right,' I said.

'And you're not supposed to say anything, right?'

'Right,' said Pip. 'If you hear us calling out you take no notice at all – it means we're breaking the rules. Because we've got fed up with looking, probably. You just carry on in your hiding-place, right?'

'Right,' said Nicky, happily.

'One,' I said.

'What?'

'Two.'

'Have you —'

'Three.'

'— started counting?'

'Four.'

'You have started counting! The game's begun. And it's my turn to hide.'

'Five.'

Squeaking with delight, Nicky scuttled off. We sighed with relief. 'Six,' I said.

This time we got to a hundred without any interruptions. 'Let's get going, then,' said Pip. 'Slowly.'

'Slowly, yes,' I nodded.

We didn't want to find Nicky too soon. If we had to go over the rules any more times, we'd go barmy. Besides, Mum and Dad were always telling us to let Nicky win when we played together. 'You're big,' they said. 'She's little. Give her a chance, can't you? It's only fair.'

OK, then. We'd be fair.

It was the slowest Geronimo I can ever remember.

We mooched through the woods, slashing at the greenery with our sticks as if we were sword-fighters under attack. Or we blew on folded grass-blades to make the rudest noise we could. Or we just yelled at the top of our voices. The idea was to give Nicky

plenty of warning to keep herself under cover. Every so often we'd stop in our tracks and swing round to face the way we'd come, or we'd make a sudden lunge into the undergrowth. Always we were on the alert not to notice Nicky the instant we got a glimpse of her. It was the best chance we'd ever given her.

At first it was fun, too.

Then it got boring.

Mainly because there was no sign of Nicky at all. At last Pip snapped his stick across his knee and sent both halves spinning into the trees. 'Where is she?' he demanded.

'Dunno.'

'Let's look properly.'

'OK.'

We'd soon find her now. A six year old can't possibly keep clear of two Geronimo experts, aged ten. Nicky'd had all the chance she was going to get. We narrowed our eyes, dropped to a half crouch and fanned out to the right and left of the path.

Half an hour later we were still looking.

Also we were getting tired. When we met up by the hollow tree at the far end of the wood we glared at each other grumpily. 'She's doing it on purpose,' I sniffed.

'Of course she is,' said Pip.

'What?'

'She's playing Geronimo.'

'Yeah, but . . .'

But what? That's exactly what Nicky was doing. Better than us, too. A six year old beating us at

Geronimo! 'Where shall we look now, Pip?' I asked crossly.

'Where we've already looked.'

'What's the point of that when we know she isn't there.'

'Because there's nowhere else we can look, Kath. We've covered the whole wood.'

'All of it?'

Pip nodded grimly. Sweat beaded his forehead. Also he was chewing his lip and I knew what that meant. 'You worried?' I asked.

'Aren't you?'

'Maybe a bit. I reckon she's back towards Mum and Dad – where we started off. We weren't playing Geronimo properly then because we were giving her a chance. She's found some place we missed, that's all.'

'Probably,' said Pip. He didn't sound very convinced.

Neither was I by the time we'd back-tracked almost as far as the car-park. We'd checked the other boundaries, too – zigzagging across a hundred yards of late autumn greenery from the main road on one side of us to the airfield's tall wire fence on the other. We were both calling out now. 'Nicky! Nicky!'

'Nicky – you've won.'

'You're the winner, Nicky.'

'We give up, Nicky! The game's over!'

'Nicky!'

'Nicky!'

'Nicky – you've beaten us! You can call out

"Geronimo" if you like!'

All we could hear was the noise we were making ourselves.

Then suddenly . . . 'Pip! Kath!'

I felt my stomach lurch with relief. 'We've found her,' I exclaimed.

'We haven't,' said Pip. 'That was Mum's voice.'

'Kathy! Pip!'

Dad's voice, too. 'Where's Nicky?' they said together as soon as they saw us.

It didn't take long to explain.

The look on their faces when we'd finished told us how serious it was. I'd rather have been moaned at or given the good hiding we were always promised when we got into worse trouble than usual. Instead Dad just said, 'An hour? She's been gone an hour, you say?'

We nodded miserably. 'Joe?' Mum whispered.

Dad shook his head. 'Maybe she's fallen asleep, Viv. Or tripped and knocked herself out.'

'Joe?'

'Don't panic. That won't help a bit. It's only a small wood so let's search it one last time. You take the airfield side, I'll go towards the main road. Keep shouting and keep your eyes skinned. If she doesn't turn up . . .'

Dad blinked and looked away. This was too much for Mum. 'You do the looking, Joe,' she snapped. 'Pip and Kath can help you. Panic or not, it's the police station for me. I don't care if I do look a fool. I'll take the car.'

Before we could argue, she was off.

Dumbly, I watched her – I'd never seen Mum running full pelt before. Her sandals went flap-flap-flap against the bottom of her feet as she crunched across the gravel, sending little spurts of dust and grit up around her ankles. I heard Dad saying something to me. 'Sorry?' I said.

'Wait here, Kath,' he repeated. 'Nicky might come back.'

Might come back?

Only might?

Did Dad think . . .

I wanted to stop the world at that moment – to freeze-frame the whole scene, like on our video at home, with Dad and Pip in mid-step as they plunged back into the woods, Mum reaching towards the car and Nicky still safe somewhere, giggling quietly to herself because she hadn't been found.

Please God Please God Please God.

Just for a split-second it did seem I'd slowed things down, too. Then we were back to normal speed again as Mum wrenched open the car door and stooped to get in. Instantly, from the back seat, came a shrill piping voice. Nicky's voice.

GERONIMO!

Mum didn't know the rules, obviously. Otherwise she wouldn't have hoiked Nicky out on to the gravel by the scruff of her neck and smacked her hard across the

back of the legs, all in the same movement.

Poor Nicky!

As we drove home, though, with Mum and Dad going on and on and on at us over their shoulders about jokes that weren't a bit funny, our little sister slumped between Pip and me wearing a smug look on her tear-stained face. OK, so she got it wrong again at the end by calling out. All right, so it had earned her a hefty clump. Fair enough, so her big brother and sister were refusing to talk to her. She was still the winner at Geronimo.

And she'd never let us forget it.

7   A Family Secret – Part II

Why did Dad pick Hallowe'en to tell us? Later, he reckoned the actual date was just a fluke – he simply couldn't keep the secret any longer. But wouldn't it have been kinder to wait till a more normal day? As it was, Nicky was dressed up in a witch's costume with blacked-out teeth and flour in her hair, Pip had a weird, stitched-together look because he was supposed to be Frankenstein's monster and I was a ghost.

A pretty solid ghost, admittedly.

More like the kind that knocks down walls rather than walks through them. I had a white sheet over the top of my duffel coat, you see, so I wouldn't catch cold trick-or-treating along the street.

'How did the party go?' Mum asked us as we came in the back door.

'T'riffic,' Nicky said.

'Except for Nelson's Eye,' sniggered Pip.

'Nelson's Eye?' said Mum. 'You didn't play that old game, did you?'

'You bet,' I said.

'Don't tell her,' Nicky sulked.

'Don't tell me what?' Mum asked.

'Don't,' said Nicky, stamping her foot.

From the scowl on her face, you'd think she was about to cast a spell on all three of us. Not that Mum was very scared. We could see her checking out the situation. 'Something to do with Nelson's Eye?' she asked.

'Stupid game,' Nicky scowled.

Pip and I were trying really hard not to laugh at her. After all, Nelson's Eye is pretty spooky even for a big kid. I'd gone all goose-pimply, too, when they put the blindfold on me. 'This is Nelson's missing arm,' they always say as they guide your hand along the empty sleeve. 'And this is the black patch he wore over his missing eye,' they go on, steering your fingertips across the face of the kid pretending to be Nelson. 'And this is the missing eye itself . . .'

Eeek!

Is it a specially-peeled grape?

Or a curled-up slug?

Or maybe an actual popped-out-of-its-socket eye?

Nelson's Eye?

Every year I shuddered just the same. No wonder Nicky had gone on screaming and screaming and screaming. It was her first time, after all. We'd taken ages to calm her down.

Mum seemed to understand what had happened without being told. Straight away she put her arms round Nicky. 'Apart from Nelson's Eye, though . . .' she said. 'You had a good time, did you?'

'T'riffic,' sniffed Nicky.

'But tiring,' said Mum. 'If those yawns are anything to go by.'

For once even Nicky didn't argue about being sent to bed ahead of us. Behind her, she left a trail of witch as she climbed upstairs – her pointed hat, her broomstick, her spellbook. 'Come and kiss me,' she called to Mum from the landing.

'Night, Nicky,' we called.

'Another Hallowe'en over,' I said. 'Firework Night next.'

'Have a heart,' said Mum. 'It's one thing after another with you lot. You'll be talking about Christmas soon.'

'Yeah!' said Pip. 'Jingle-bells, jingle-bells . . . '

'What's up, Mum?' I interrupted him.

Pip had missed the look on her face. 'What's up?' he repeated anxiously.

'Nothing,' said Mum.

She'd bent down to fuss with the oven though there wasn't anything cooking that I could see. 'Your dad would like a word with you,' she said. 'He's in the other room.'

'Have we been naughty?' said Pip.

'Not that I've heard,' Mum said. 'He just wants . . . a word, that's all.'

'About us?' I said.

Mum turned, half smiling and half frowning. 'A bit about you,' she said. 'Off you go.' She was still fiddling with the oven as we left her.

Pip stopped me at the door of the sitting-room. 'What's he want?' he hissed.

'How should I know?'

'You do though. I can see you do.'

'Maybe . . .'

'Tell me, then.'

I bit my lip. Had he really forgotten the day of the water-bombs? 'Only maybe,' I said.

'Yeah?' glared Pip.

But I wasn't being awkward, honestly. I couldn't have explained what I knew. I just knew it. Especially when I saw Dad.

He was still in his British Rail uniform even though his shift must've been finished hours ago. Something else was odd, too. Over in the corner the television screen was blank. Was Dad really missing 'The Nine O'Clock News'? Instead, on his lap, was the wedding album. And on the arm of the big old armchair where Mum usually sat he had a glass of whisky.

Whisky?

And it wasn't even his birthday?

I felt Pip bump up against me and his fingers close over mine. We waited for Dad to speak. 'Pip,' he said, eventually. 'Kath . . .'

'Yes, Dad?'

'Yes?'

Dad cleared his throat and looked down. He shut the wedding album and slipped it behind the arm of the chair. The room was so quiet I could hear the tick of the clock on the mantelpiece – for the first time ever when other people were in the room. Usually I only heard it when I was alone, reading. 'I've . . . I've got something to tell you,' Dad said. 'I want . . . I want you to be very grown-up. You must listen carefully. Really carefully. OK?'

We both nodded. 'Good,' said Dad.

He licked his lips. 'It's about your mum,' he went on. 'Your *real* mum, I mean.'

'Our real mum?' Pip said.

'In a way, son.'

Dad gave a shrug as if he couldn't quite believe what he was saying. Or as if, now he was saying it, it didn't sound right even to him. 'You see, I've been married before. I've had two weddings. Your real mum was the first one. She died soon after you twins

were born. Never left the hospital. So there was no chance for her to *be* your mum, properly speaking. In another way, *that's* your real mum out there in the kitchen.'

'Our *step*-mother,' I said.

'Shut up!' Pip hissed.

'Your step-mother, yes,' Dad nodded. 'But she's looked after you for six years or more, Kath. That's real, too.'

'But she didn't actually have us,' I said stubbornly. 'In the hospital, I mean. Like when she had Nicky. Is that what you're saying, Dad?'

'That's right.'

'Why didn't you tell us before?' Pip asked.

Dad sat back a moment, closing his eyes. I'd never seen him like this. His uniform was as smart as ever in the lamplight, but where was the cheery sorter-out of stroppiness on the Inter-City Express? He looked so shy.

At last he spoke. 'My fault,' he said. 'Viv – your mum out there – she wanted me to. She wanted you to know from the beginning. But I kept on putting it off. It got easier and easier to forget, I suppose. To pretend it never happened. Especially when Nicky came along and you all got on so well together. Also . . . also you seemed to me to have enough on your plate, all three of you.' He meant the white kids who sneered at us because we weren't quite white and the black kids because we weren't quite black.

'You always stick up for us, Dad,' Pip said.

'Always.'

'I hope so, Pip.' Dad was looking up at him gratefully. 'Your other mum – the one who died – didn't have any family at all apart from an older brother who went to Canada years ago. So why rake up the past anyway, I thought? Viv always said I was wrong. You had a right to know, she reckoned. Reckoned I was stupid too, because you were sure to find out eventually.'

'Cousin Vernon,' I said bitterly.

'What?'

I shook my head. It wasn't worth explaining now. 'Will you tell us about her?' Pip asked. 'Our . . . our other mum, that is?'

'One day, yes.'

'Not today?'

'Not today, no.'

They were both trying to smile now. Don't ask me what was supposed to be funny. Just imagine the picture we made: a railway guard, Frankenstein's monster and a ghost. We'd have stayed like that forever, I think, if a voice hadn't called round the door. 'Can anyone crash this party? Or do you have to be in a funny costume?'

'Hello, Mum,' said Pip at once.

'Hello,' I whispered.

I hadn't turned round but I knew it was me she'd come to. 'Must be a bit of a shock,' she murmured in my ear. 'You were bound to take it hardest, Kath. Feel bad, do you?'

'Like Nelson's flippin' eye,' I snarled.

And burst into tears.

To my surprise, Pip didn't tease me at all. He let me have first taste of Dad's whisky as well which we both pretended was terrific. After that, though it was long past our bedtime, we watched television for a while with Pip on Dad's lap and me on Mum's. It got so late, and I was so sleepy, I don't even remember being carried upstairs or taking off my ghost outfit or Mum kissing me good-night.

Even if you feel better afterwards, being let in on a Family Secret certainly tires you out.

8   Sweeney Ted

His name was Miss Maynard's fault.

One afternoon – to wake us all up, I suppose – she suddenly launched into the story of someone she called The Demon Barber of Fleet Street. She reckoned he cut people's throats instead of their hair so he could sell them as meat to the pie-shop next door. 'And you know how they finally caught this dreadful man?' Miss Maynard asked.

'No, miss.'

'A toe-nail,' she said. 'Yes, a human toe-nail. It was found in one of the pies.'

'Yuk!' we all went.

'So don't forget his name, children. It's quite famous. He was called . . .'

Everyone bent forward to catch her whisper. 'Sweeney Todd.'

'Sweeney Ted, she means,' said Pip at once.

And the whole class burst out laughing, which didn't please Miss Maynard a bit. She made Pip stay in at playtime to clean out the gerbil's cage, a job everyone hated.

85

After this, though, Mr O'Carroll was known as Sweeney Ted forever.

He had the salon at the end of our street, you see. TED J. O'CARROLL – MODERN UNISEX HAIRSTYLING said his shop sign. And every kid in the neighbourhood had to go there partly because Ted knew all of our parents and partly because he was so cheap. Not that we had anything against his actual haircuts. Sweeney Ted could do skinheads, mohicans, Afro, the wet look . . . anything you liked that your mum and dad allowed. No problem there. What drove us all screwy were Sweeney Ted's questions.

Every visit was the same.

Once Sweeney Ted had found out what you wanted and settled you back in his chair with a white sheet half choking you and your feet dangling about a mile from the floor, he'd ask 'Comfy?'

'Fine,' you'd say.

Apart from little matters like cramp, pins and needles and not being able to breathe. But worse was on its way because the instant Ted started to snip, the test would begin. 'Seven eights?' he'd rap out.

'Fifty-six.'

'Eight nines?'

'Seventy-two.'

'What?'

'Seventy-two.'

'Thought I'd caught you there.'

And Ted would give a brisk laugh as if you hadn't fooled *him* by changing your answer but just this once

86

he'd let you get away with it. 'How about eleven twelves, then?'

'A hundred and thirty-two.'

'And seven sevens?'

'Fourteen.'

'Sorry?'

'Fourteen.'

You'd got it wrong on purpose, of course, being fed up already with the whole thing. This was a mistake, though. In the mirror in front of you you'd see a big grin spread across Sweeney Ted's face. 'Seven sevens are fourteen?' he'd snort. 'You're well off-beam!'

And he'd recite all of the seven times table so fast you couldn't keep up with him. His lips were just a blur as he towered over you with his comb and scissors poised above your head like torture instruments ready to stab if you had another slip-up.

At least stabbing would have put you out of your misery.

For it wasn't just your tables you were expected to remember. Sweeney Ted would test you on the Kings, Queens and Prime Ministers of British History, on the capitals of every country in the world, on the name and place of each planet in the solar system . . . and on whatever else had caught his fancy since your last visit. 'Know what a marsupial is?' he'd ask. 'Saw a piece on the telly about 'em.'

'So did I.'

'Let's see what you've forgotten then . . .'

And he'd force you through the whole thing word by

word. At other times he'd say something like, 'E = mc². Know why that's important?'

'No.'

'Heard it on this radio programme. Listen, while I explain . . .'

Which he always did – over and over again till your jaw ached from keeping your screams locked in.

The funny thing was, Sweeney Ted didn't do all this for the usual grown-up's reason. Never once did he tell you how duff your school was compared with the one he went to as a kid. More the other way round, actually. He'd say things like, 'Knows a lot, that Miss Maynard of yours. Yes, I realise she's a bit old-fashioned, a bit of a battleaxe, you give her a chance. Even that old Mrs Roper's got her head screwed on right. Take advantage of it while you can. That's my advice.'

'We will, Mr O'Carroll.'

'Make sure you do. What are nine nines, by the way? Come on, come on – should have the answer on the tip of your tongue at your age. Miss Maynard would have a fit if she could see the way you're dithering.'

'I wasn't dithering,' you wanted to shout. 'I was trying to get a word in edgeways, you stupid four-eyed gasbag!' But you didn't, of course. Not with your dad seeing Sweeney Ted at the pub practically every weekend.

So no wonder Pip and I moaned when Dad sent us to Ted's for our pre-Christmas trim. 'Yes, I know you'd prefer one of those fancy glass-and-spotlight joints in the High Street,' he said. 'But Ted O'Carroll gives you just as good a job for less than half the money. Besides . . .'

Besides, Sweeney Ted's old mum had just died. This is what Dad meant. Ted had been mooching about like a spare part ever since the funeral so now wasn't the time to take our custom away.

'What if we were to put our pocket-money towards it?' I said desperately. 'Could we go somewhere different, then?'

'Sorry, Kath.'

'But Ted's such a pain, Dad!'

'A pain?' Dad's lips went all tight. 'It's not easy when you've lost someone close to you, Kath. We've all been rallying round Ted a bit lately. Maybe he has been taking it badly, but he'll soon be back to normal. And we'll have a bit less of the "Ted" while we're on the subject. He's Mr O'Carroll to you.'

'But nobody calls him Mr O'Carroll, Dad,' I protested.

'You do,' said Dad grimly.

'I do, too,' Nicky piped up. 'I like Mr O'Carroll, Dad. He cut my hair last week. He's a nice man.'

'Glad somebody appreciates him,' Dad said.

And that was the end of that. We couldn't even get our own back on our creepy-crawly little sister. Five minutes later Dad had pushed us out of the house. 'Get a move on,' he warned. 'Otherwise Ted will have shut up shop before you get there.'

We should be so lucky.

Gloomily, Pip kicked a stone across the pavement. 'Reckon it'll be tests over and over again?'

'Why should this visit be any different?' I shrugged.

Our only hope was to make sure we had our brains properly in gear. Seven *sevens* are forty-nine. Queen Victoria reigned from *1837 to 1901*. *Berne* is the capital of Switzerland. The furthest planet in the solar system is *Pluto*. *Marsupials* are . . . $E = mc^2$ means . . . Yuk!

TING!

As usual the bell on Sweeney Ted's door reminded me of the start of a boxing-match. We took a deep breath and went in. 'Hello, Mr O'Carroll,' we said together.

'Hello, Satchwell twins.'

Like fighters touching gloves, I thought.

Already Pip and I were trying to make way for each other so we didn't have to go first. I won for a change. This meant it was up to me to keep the score. Not that Pip would ever beat Sweeney Ted. He always won in the end just by wearing you out. A technical knock-out, we called it. I picked up a teenage magazine I knew backwards from previous visits and pretended to read. Any second now the contest would start.

Except it didn't.

To our surprise, Sweeney Ted said nothing.

Not a word.

After he'd checked it was a trim we were after, the only sound that he made came from the snip-and-click, snip-and-click of his scissors and comb. It was

weird – like a clock you've heard all your life suddenly
without a tick any more or hiccups that vanish just
when you get used to them. What was the matter with
him? His eyes looked as bright and brainy as they
always did behind his huge spectacles. And his shock
of sandy hair made him seem more than ever like a
mad scientist. Why so silent then? Was he still missing
his mum? 'Finished, Pip,' he said suddenly.

Pip pulled a face at me as we changed places.

I could hardly bear it. 'Ask me a question,' I wanted
to say. 'Any question you like, Mr O'Carroll. I promise I won't get it right.'

Still he didn't speak. Not till I'd settled myself, more or less, slumped so far down in the chair all I could see of me in the mirror was the top of my head. Then at last came that brisk clearing of the throat, we knew so well. 'Er . . . Kath?' he asked.

'Yes?'

'How's school?'

'Fine,' I said eagerly.

'You're getting good marks with Miss Maynard? You and Pip, I mean?'

'Fine.'

'In all subjects would you say? Across the board like?'

'Fine, yes.'

'Good. That's good. That's very . . .'

'Good?'

'What?'

'Nothing,' I said hastily.

I heard Pip snigger but I wasn't really being cheeky. Just filling a gap, that's all. And there was plenty of gaps to fill because Sweeney Ted's chat stopped right there. He went straight back to snip-snip, click-click snip-snip . . .

What was he thinking about?

I could see from his reflection in the mirror that he had more on his mind than Prime Ministers, capital cities and the solar system. Was he trying to decide something? Sooner than I expected, he laid down his comb and scissors and whisked away the sheet. A no-question haircut is certainly nippy. 'Thanks, Mr

O'Carroll,' I said. 'Let's go, Pip.'

'Hold on a mo',' said Sweeney Ted.

'What?'

'No rush is there?'

'Oh, sorry,' I said. 'Here's your money, Mr O'Carroll.'

'Mine, too,' said Pip.

Sweeney Ted shook his head. 'It's not the money. You can keep that.'

'Keep it?'

'For Christmas presents. You'd like that, would you?'

Pip and I looked at each other blankly. Behind his glasses Sweeney Ted's eyes were brighter than ever. He coughed, scratched an itch under his chin and smiled awkwardly. 'Call it wages,' he went on. 'For a little job I'd like you to do.'

'Us?' said Pip.

'Both of you, yes. More a favour than a job, actually. I want your advice, you see. You being such good students and all.'

'Students?'

'According to your dad. Right proud of you, he is. Says the pair of you are specially smart when it comes to words. That's true, is it? You can put a few words together on paper, can you?'

'I suppose we can,' said Pip.

'What do you want us to do?' I asked.

'Help me with a letter.'

'A letter?'

'A letter saying thank you – so I can send it to all the people who've been so kind to me since my old mum . . . passed on. Your dad, for instance. I've *said* thank you, of course. But that's not the same as a letter, is it?'

'Suppose not,' Pip said.

'A letter's better, probably,' I agreed.

Sweeney Ted nodded. 'That's my opinion. The trouble is . . . I'm not much of a fist at writing. I'm a number man, myself. That and facts. Never forget a fact, I don't. Facts and numbers – they're meat and drink to me. Once heard, always remembered.'

With a long hairdressy finger he tapped his forehead. 'You've noticed that, I expect.'

'We have, yes.'

'Take a pride in numbers and facts, I do. But not writing. Writing's a bit of a weak spot. Always was. I've made a start, though.'

From his pocket he took a folded sheet of paper. 'See?' he said.

At the top, in letters so big and wobbly he must have had both hands on the pencil, was his address. At the bottom, copied out in block capitals, was TED. J. O'CARROLL – MODERN UNISEX HAIRSTYLING. 'It's the bit in between where I need help,' he explained. 'I know what I want to say.'

It didn't take long. All I had to do was write down what he dictated, really. Afterwards, Pip made a list of the people Ted needed to thank and we both showed him where to copy in the names. 'Bless you, Satchwell twins,' he said. 'I appreciate it.'

We didn't talk much on the way home. Instead we stared at the Christmas lights in all the windows and jingled the haircut money in our pockets. It was a lot more than we'd got carol-singing the night before.

At our front gate, though, Pip finally said what we were thinking. 'Just fancy, Kath. Test after flippin' test driving us potty every visit and all the time Sweeney Ted couldn't write.'

'Read,' I said. 'It's reading he can't do.'

'Reading?'

'It's why he gets everything from the telly and the radio. Or learns it by heart.'

'Yeah,' Pip nodded. 'That's what it is.'

What we didn't say, what we didn't need to say, was that if the other kids in Miss Maynard's class – or any class in the school come to that – ever found out about Sweeney Ted's secret, it wouldn't be from us.

9   Pictures In Our Eyes

'Pictures in my eyes,' Nicky called them. She was talking about dreams, of course. They fascinated us. We discussed our special ones over and over again – sometimes for so long there wasn't any time left to hear one of my bedtime stories. This never really bothered me, though, because dreams are a kind of story in a way.

Do you have any you can't forget?

We did.

Pip's was the spookiest. 'It always goes like this,' he said. 'I'm lying in bed right here – like I am now. There's moonlight coming through the windows, spilling over the bedcover and glinting in the wardrobe mirror. You two are sound asleep. I can hear you breathing . . . breathing.

'Suddenly I fall out of bed – don't ask me how, I just do. I roll over and . . . OOPS! Instead of bashing myself on the floor, though, which is what I'm expecting, I'm not hurt at all. Not even a bruise. You want to know why?'

'Why?' asked Nicky and me together.

'Because I never hit the floor.'

'Eh?' said Nicky.

'How come?' I asked.

Pip gave a laugh that was more puzzled than funny. 'Because I'm caught before I reach the floor. Caught, yes. By four little men.'

'Little men?' Nicky squealed.

'Four of them, yes. They're about as high as the seat of a chair and they catch me by my hands and feet – I fall in a sort of star-shape, you see.'

'What happens next?'

'Kath, something really peculiar. All they do is swing me backwards and forwards . . . gently, gently . . . backwards and forwards. Like I was being given slow-motion bumps on my birthday – except it's not up and down, it's from side to side. Then, exactly together, they let go. And I kind of drift back into bed. That's all.'

'*All*?' exclaimed Nicky.

I knew what she meant. I'd got a creepy feeling, too. Especially when Pip said he'd had this dream often.

For ages, while all the laughing and chatter from Mum and Dad's New Year party downstairs floated up to us, we argued about who the little men were. Goblins? Trolls? Hobbits, maybe?

None of these were quite right, Pip reckoned. The trouble was, he couldn't really tell us what the men looked like. Apparently he could only see them – any of them – out of the corner of his eye.

This was the trouble with Pictures in Your Eyes, we

decided. Somehow it's only out of the *corner* of your eye you ever do get to see them.

Next was my turn. I knew exactly the dream I wanted to share. 'Clapham Junction,' I said.

'Clapham Junction?' said Pip. 'That's a railway station, isn't it?'

'The busiest in the world, Dad reckons.'

'How come you dream about that?'

'Dunno.'

Pretty soon they knew why I'd chosen it, though. I was frightened all over again, just describing it. 'I've got to cross the railway tracks,' I said. 'Loads of them – stretching for miles in either direction. Only they're big tracks – knee high, almost, and wide as a diving board. Some of them are live, too.'

'Live?' wailed Nicky.

'Not live like we are,' Pip explained. 'She means live with electricity. If you touch them you go bang like a firework and that's the end of you.'

'So it's not easy,' I went on. 'I've got to stretch my legs across each of them, near the sleepers . . .'

'Sleepers?'

'Not that sort of sleeper,' groaned Pip. 'Kath means the planks of wood laid on the gravel between the rails. Keep quiet, Nicky. Give her a chance to get going. I want to hear this.'

So did I.

I was keen to find out if I could make my twin brother and my little sister sweat with terror the way I always did when I had this dream.

100

Whether I managed it or not, I can't say. I was too busy describing the trains as they flashed past – CLICKETTY - THUD, CLICKETTY - THUD, CLICKETTY - THUD – only just in front of me or only just behind me. They were so close I got train-stink in my nostrils and train-dust in my hair. Would they zap me next time?

Or would I stumble on to a live rail first?

On and on I went, high-stepping over the tracks, expecting any second to be sizzled or crunched or both. 'The worst thing is I never do find out if I get across,' I said. 'The dream sort of fades away . . .'

'Wow!' said Nicky faintly.

'Think I'll travel by bus from now on,' Pip muttered.

For a while we lay there, picturing little men and railway tracks. We'd almost forgotten how fed up we were at being in bed at all. I mean, it *was* New Year's Eve. OK, so Mum and Dad did want a grown-ups-only party, for once, but what about us? Why should we be left out? Were we the only kids in the world who'd actually been put to bed *early*?

Still, we felt better now we'd had a good natter.

A bit, anyway.

Pip turned over and reached across to the window, twitching back the curtain. Outside, from what we could see through the frost on the pane, it was very midnight-ish. 'Can't be long now,' said Pip. 'We'll hear the chimes on the Town Hall clock, I expect. And all the boats sounding their hooters on the river. Then

101

we'll know it's Next Year. Let's keep quiet till it happens.'

'Not fair,' Nicky wailed at once.

'What isn't?'

'My dream,' she said. 'You haven't listened to my dream. It's about a fifty pence piece.'

'A fifty pence piece?' I sniggered. 'Terrific.'

'Let her tell it,' said Pip.

He was right, I admit. But how good can a six year old's dream be? It would spoil the atmosphere we'd built up, never mind maybe cutting across midnight. 'Shall I tell it, Kath?' asked Nicky, shyly.

'OK,' I sighed.

'It'll be good,' Nicky said.

To my surprise, it was good. There wasn't much to it but Pip and I understood exactly the way Nicky felt. 'It's this fifty pence piece,' she said. 'I get given it in my dream but I know I'm dreaming. So I hold on to it really tight 'cos I want to go to the shops and spend it when I wake up. Really, really tight I hold it.'

'What happens?' Pip asked.

'When I wake up, you mean?'

'Yes.'

Nicky gave a heavy sigh. 'My hand's empty,' she said.

Normally Pip and I would have laughed at this. Something told us she hadn't finished, though. 'So next time . . . next time I decide I'm going to hold on so tight I'll crumble it to bits, practically. Extra-extra-extra tight. And I do. I can feel my finger-

nails sticking right in my hand round the fifty pence. Really sticking in. Then I wake up.'

I cleared my throat. 'Is it there?'

'No,' said Nicky.

We heard her shift on to her elbows. It was too dark for us to be sure but she seemed to be staring down at her hand. Then she spoke again. 'But when I look, in the morning I mean, in abroad daylight—'

'Broad daylight,' I said. 'Not abroad daylight.'

'Shut up,' snapped Pip. 'Tell it your way, Nicky. Go on.'

'There isn't much to go on with,' Nicky said. 'Except that . . .'

'Yes?'

'Well, in my hand – in my real-life hand, Pip, which I really, really am looking at – I can see the marks left by my fingernails.'

This really did shut me up. Pip, too. In fact, it shut us all up. I mean, if a dream fist can become a real fist why can't a dream fifty pence piece . . . no. No, it didn't make sense. 'That sort of thing only happens in stories,' I said.

'Yeah,' Nicky said.

'It could happen in a dream as well, Kath,' Pip pointed out. 'A nice dream, sort of. You know, the kind where a clock goes backwards so we end up not missing a New Year's Party, for instance.'

'Maybe we'd better go to sleep, then,' I said in disgust. 'So we can dream.'

Downstairs, as if to tease us, there was a sudden

104

burst of laughter. Dad telling a joke, probably. It made us more determined than ever to stay awake.

If we could.

I should've known better, I suppose, from last time. Staying awake on purpose while you're actually in bed is pretty nearly impossible – even with music thumping below you from the Satchwell New Year Party and the night about to go mad with bells, hooters and people banging dustbin lids. As the seconds ticked away like minutes, and the minutes like hours, our talk got more and more patchy.

Soon Pip was yawning more than he spoke and Nicky was in a doze. Me, too. However hard I tried, I found myself drifting high over the railway-tracks to a dream-and-story land, full of wopsies and Dracula Dust and wedding albums where four little men helped Ms Dixon and Sweeney Ted beat us at Geronimo . . .

'Kath?'

'Wha . . .'

'Kath?'

'Is it midnight?' I mumbled.

'Midnight?' Mum laughed. She was standing in the doorway wearing a party-hat. 'Midnight's ages away yet,' she said. 'Pip and Nicky have been up for nearly an hour, though. You were so sound asleep we thought we'd leave you here a bit longer. Ready for the party, Kath?'

'The party?'

'The party, yes. It *is* New Year's Eve, you know!'

I sat up in a flurry of bedclothes. 'You meant us to come, then? All along?'

'Of course, we did. We only pretended to leave you out so you'd get some sleep first. Remember what happened last year? You three were so tired we had to put you to bed before the party was over. Come on, Kath. Get dressed quickly so we can join in the fun. Half the street's downstairs . . . is something the matter, love?'

'Nothing, no.'

'Then don't rub your eyes so hard. Got something in them, have you?'

'Only pictures, Mum,' I said.

Challenge in the Dark

Robert Leeson

Mike Baxter's first day at his new school marks the start of an unforgettable and challenging week – not least when he makes an enemy of Steven Taylor and his bullying older brother, Spotty Sam. Mike's friends "help out" by setting up a dare for both him and his enemy Steven Taylor – to stay in an old disused underground shelter. Before either has much time to protest they find themselves exposed to real dangers, experiencing fear and panic as a result of more than playground victimization.

"This short adventure has the same unmistakable veracity and friendly humour that has made *The Demon Bike Rider* so popular with young readers."
Growing Point

The Demon Bike Rider and *Wheel of Danger* are also in Young Lions.

The Fiend Next Door

Sheila Lavelle

Charlie Ellis lives next door to Angela Mitchell whom she once described in a class essay as 'My Best Fiend'. Living next to Angela is a mixed blessing. Angela has the most remarkable ideas and somehow Charlie always seems to get involved. The trouble is that Angela's plans have a horrible habit of going badly wrong and more often than not it seems to be Charlie who ends up getting the blame. It was, after all, Angela who borrowed the baby and pretended that she had kidnapped it but it was Charlie who got landed with looking after it – and trying to put it back. Also Angela is not above a little deviousness when it suits her. She certainly stopped at nothing to get her hands on the bag that Charlie had been given though, in the end, Charlie got her own back with vengeance.

Terrible though Angela can be, Charlie has to admit that life would be very dull without her around.

Also in Lions are *My Best Fiend* and *Trouble with the Fiend*.

Simon and the Witch

Margaret Stuart Barry

Simon's friend the witch lives in a neat, semi-detached house with a television and a telephone, but she has never heard of Christmas or been to the seaside. However, she has a wand, which she loses, causing confusion at the local constabulary, and a mean-looking cat called George, who eats the furniture when she forgets to feed him. The witch shows Simon how to turn the school gardener into a frog, and she and her relations liven up a hallowe'en party to the delight of the children and the alarm of the local dignitaries. With a witch for a friend, Simon discovers, life is never dull.

Very highly recommended by ILEA's *Contact* magazine: '. . . who could resist such a lively character?'

You will find more adventures of Simon and the Witch in *The Return of the Witch*, and *The Witch of Monopoly Manor* and *The Witch on Holiday*, all in Lions.

Mists and Magic

edited by Dorothy Edwards

This is a wonderful collection of stories written by favourite authors especially for this book. Dorothy Edwards brings together spells and charms, witches and mermaids, the creatures of the other world and the unexpected encounters that are the stuff of magic.

"Dorothy Edwards is a master storyteller who knows just what is guaranteed to appeal." *Books for Your Children*

Cat Walk

Mary Stolz

illustrated by Erik Blegvad

Right from the start the little black barn kitten with the enormous white paws was different from the others. He also had aspirations. He wanted a name. He gets one from young Missy, the farmer's daughter, and a home. But when she dresses him up in dolls' clothes and takes him for rides in the pram, it's time to move on – to another home.

This is an old story, disarmingly told, of a cat's progress from pillar to post, and beautifully illustrated.

All these books are available at your local bookshop or newsagent, or can be ordered from the publishers.

To order direct from the publishers just tick the titles you want and fill in the form below:

Name _____

Address _____

_____

Send to: Collins Children's Cash Sales
PO Box 11
Falmouth
Cornwall
TR10 9EN

Please enclose a cheque or postal order or debit my Visa/Access –

Credit card no:

Expiry date:

Signature:

– to the value of the cover price plus:

UK: 80p for the first book, and 20p per copy for each additional book ordered to a maximum charge of £2.00.

BFPO: 80p for the first book, and 20p per copy for each additional book.

Overseas and Eire: £1.50 for the first book, £1.00 for the second book, thereafter 30p per book.

Young Lions